MW01121429

Rope Enough is a p.,— —
two young effeminate gay party boys whose ꙮꙮꙮꙮ.... tly
interrupted when they are both charged with the murder of Ichabod's
parents. In prison, they are interviewed by right wing-journalist Cecilia
Wainscott, who quickly discovers that Ichabod is a complex character—
both a theoretical mathematician and an exuberantly dark misanthrope.
In the end, Cecilia learns a little bit about herself, gay men, theoretical
mathematics and the nature of the universe. Are Dylan and Ichabod evil
cold-blooded killers (as in Hitchcock's "Rope"), turned on by a perverse
cocktail of death and orgasms, or are they simply misunderstood by
a homophobic culture? It's all very scary and funny—but only you, the
viewer, can decide…

———

*"The dialogue is sharp and often witty… all these narrative statements
finally come together to make some provocative statements about the nature
of identity—gay or otherwise—in today's society."*
—Richard Ouzounian, *Toronto Star*

———

*"The boys and girls at the Buddies box office have their work cut out for
them in Sky Gilbert's* Rope Enough. *There will be bums in seats for
Gilbert's latest, a fully realized and compelling departure from his other
work."* —Kate Pedersen, *NOW* Magazine

———

*"An equally swank duo, disciples of Derrida, murder or claim to have
murdered for a kaleidoscope of reasons. Maybe they want to subvert
conventional ideas about gays; maybe they want to confirm them; maybe
they want to have fun. The author-director, as capricious as they are, plays
with all the possibilities, to surprisingly provocative effect."*
—Robert Cushman, *National Post*

ROPE ENOUGH

Rope Enough

Sky Gilbert

Playwrights Canada Press
Toronto • Canada

Playwrights Canada Press
The Canadian Drama Publisher
215 Spadina Avenue, Suite 230, Toronto, Ontario CANADA M5T 2C7
416-703-0013   fax 416-408-3402
orders@playwrightscanada.com • www.playwrightscanada.com

Financial support provided by the taxpayers of Canada and Ontario through the Canada Council for the Arts and the Department of Canadian Heritage through the Book Publishing Industry Development Programme, and the Ontario Arts Council.

Front cover photo of David Tomlinson and Gavin Crawford, and back cover photo of Sky Gilbert by David Hawe.
Production Editor/Cover design: JLArt

Library and Archives Canada Cataloguing in Publication

Gilbert, Sky

  Rope enough / Sky Gilbert.

A play.

ISBN 0-88754-872-5

  I. Title.

PS8563.I4743R66 2006   C812'.54   C2006-900840-X

First edition: March 2006.
Printed and bound by AGMV Marquis at Quebec, Canada.

dedicated to Ian Jarvis

"At present, people see fogs, not because there are fogs,
but because poets and painters have taught them
the mysterious loveliness of such effects.
There may have been fogs for centuries in London.
I dare say there were. But no one saw them,
and so we did not know anything about them.
They did not exist till Art had invented them."
—Oscar Wilde, *The Decay of Lying*

Rope Enough was first produced by Buddies in Bad Times Theatre, Toronto, Ontario in April and May 2005, with the following company:

Ichabod Malframe	Gavin Crawford
Dylan Short	David Tomlinson
Cecilia Wainscott	Catherine McNally
John Trick	Ryan McVittie
Bobbi LaCreme	Patrick Conner

Directed by Sky Gilbert
Set and Lighting by Steve Lucas
Costumes by Michelle Turpin
Stage Managed by Sharon Di Genova

CHARACTERS

Ichabod Malframe	(29 years) an accused homosexual killer
Dylan Short	(27 years) an accused homosexual killer
Cecilia Wainscott	(45 years) a journalist
Bobbi LaCreme	(40 years) head of the Rainbow Channel
John Trick	(35 years) a detective

TIME

2004

PLACE

A white room: living room, prison waiting room, insane asylum.

Rope Enough

ACT ONE

Lights up on a vast white room. CECILIA sits in a stylish dining room chair at the very front of it. She seems too close to the audience.

CECILIA I worry about Bobbi. That may seem quaint to you, or old fashioned or not politically correct. But those judgments have no affect on me. They really don't. Honestly I couldn't care less. I've always lived a somewhat unconventional life and that's the way it is. On the contrary I suppose some might call it terribly conventional. That is,—to marry a very rich man. But I didn't marry Lance because he was rich. I married him because he was terribly attractive, deeply charismatic. Now he's facing fraud charges. I have no doubt he will make it through. I have absolutely no doubt at all. That's the kind of man he is; that's the kind of man I married. But nevertheless, I do worry about my dear friend, Bobbi. I worry because he goes to the gym too much, and is probably taking steroids—though he denies it, of course. I worry because he has a relationship with a younger man who is, inevitably, his intellectual inferior. I worry because he's almost forty years old and people still call him Bobbi. I worry because he is a gay man. I know that is perhaps, again not a particularly correct thing to say. But I don't care. Let's get this out of the way first. I have absolutely no sexual prejudices. I quite like sex. When Lance and I engage in it, and we still do, at our advanced ages and after nearly thirty years of marriage, I thoroughly enjoy it. And like any married couple, now and then we have our kinky side. I don't mind telling you that. I don't consider any sexual peculiarity peculiar. I don't consider any fetish bizarre. If people want to chew on old boots to bring themselves to orgasm or slide uncommonly large objects up their bottoms, I simply look on it as part of the multifaceted entity which we call our world. But, nevertheless, I worry about Bobbi. He drinks too much—so many gay men do. And there's something about the way he drinks—an edge, a desperation. Of course we all (practically all) like our glass of wine in the evening. It's not that. Perhaps it has nothing to do with being gay at all, perhaps I would worry about anybody who started as a hooker in Espagnola (please don't tell anyone I said that—it really is very much a secret), and now runs Canada's premiere—in fact only—gay television station. I worry about someone with that much ambition about someone who has, in fact, achieved so much. So I hope you will agree with me that it is natural that I worry about him. And after I tell you this story you may find yourself worrying about him too.

> *Blackout. Lights up on three tacky vinyl kitchen chairs and a kitchen table. DYLAN, ICHABOD, and JOHN enter. They are drunk and high.*

JOHN Undanceable.

DYLAN Oh don't say that, John.

JOHN It's true. I couldn't dance to it.

DYLAN Just because the DJ got lost somewhere in hip hop after Madonna.

> *They flop down in the chairs.*

JOHN And what about that guy with the whistle.

DYLAN Too many party favours.

JOHN You're not kidding. You got any beer?

DYLAN *(as ICHABOD opens it)* Ichabod was reading your mind.

ICHABOD I'm psychic.

JOHN Oooh! Brewski. *(He takes a sip.)* Where did you get that name?

ICHABOD My mother gave it to me.

DYLAN She was literary.

ICHABOD Dylan.

DYLAN She was. Why shouldn't I say she was literary?

ICHABOD *(taking out a tablet)* Would you like some E?

JOHN Jeeze. Looks tempting.

ICHABOD Looks tempting… but.

JOHN I already did a tab at home.

ICHABOD So did we. Why not do another?

JOHN I'm sailing just fine now.

ICHABOD I'd say so.

DYLAN We like the cut of your jib.

JOHN Do ya now. *(He takes off his shirt.)* And there's more where that came from.

DYLAN We can tell. We couldn't help noticing you… *(dramatically)* at the bar.

JOHN Jeeze it's hard not to notice you guys.

DYLAN We have a sort of a reputation. It's very disconcerting.

JOHN I guess it was all that buzz about last year.

DYLAN *(glancing at ICHABOD, who turns away)* Well it *could* be…

   Pause, JOHN looks around uncomfortably.

JOHN Did I say something wrong? Sorry.

DYLAN No, it's okay. *(stage whisper)* Ichabod can be a little *sensitive.*

JOHN Gee, I'm sorry, Ichabod, did I say something wrong? *(pause)*

DYLAN *You* could never say anything *wrong*, honey. It's just that… it all happened to him more than me. *(pause)* And then there's the star-fucker factor.

JOHN Oh, I get it.

DYLAN Yeah, it's so weird.

JOHN You get a lot of guys who are into that?

DYLAN Well Ichabod thinks we do.

ICHABOD Do we have to talk about this?

JOHN Hey, sorry, it was the furthest thing from my mind. I could understand how it could be like… very traumatic for you.

ICHABOD It wasn't.

JOHN *(after a pause)* No?

ICHABOD I can't tell you how fucking stupid the whole thing was.
I mean as if I was close to them, just because they were my goddamn
family. Jesus Christ my sister was fucking autistic. Do you know
what that is? And my mother and father... well they don't even
bear talking about. There's *nothing* to talk about. Except how much
I hated them. It was a fucking relief to get rid of them. Honestly. My
mother... can I tell you how stupid she was? What a fucking victim?
And my father molested me. He was a fucking faggot. I'm sure he
made me into one. Whoever killed them was doing them a fucking
favour. They were already dead. They were the walking dead. There
are some forms of living which are not... living. There is a kind of
apex of boredom and sheer innocuousness where it all becomes
about... going to the store. That's the only way I can express it.
(pause) I know I should feel guilty but I don't. *(pause)*

JOHN Guilty for what.

ICHABOD For talking about it. *(pause)* What do you think? *(pause)*

DYLAN Gee, honey, for somebody who didn't want to talk about it, you
sure talked a lot.

ICHABOD Fuck off.

DYLAN He's so sweet to me. That's why I love him, so very very much.
(pause)

JOHN You know what's really weird.

DYLAN No, honey, what. The E making you horny yet?

JOHN No. Fuck. Fuck this is weird.

DYLAN What, tell us, we'll understand. Hey nothing is too weird. You
want to sit on my face? Hey, I can totally handle it. Unless you're
a mess. *(pause)* But I'm really quite embarrassed to say, I can pretty
well handle that too.

JOHN Well the thing is.

DYLAN Oh come on darling, let it all out, like a big poo. It will be so
satisfying, afterwards.

JOHN *(hangs his head, in shame)* Jeeze.

DYLAN Oh I love it when they get embarrassed. I love it when squeaky
clean white boys get all dirty, and then feel ashamed.

JOHN You're gonna hate me.

DYLAN Goodness, are you sure you took E? It sounds more like
a crystal meth mixed with K downer to me.

JOHN No, I'm sorry, it's just... you know what the rumour on the street
is.

>   *Pause, ICHABOD looks at him, evenly.*

ICHABOD Oh, that we killed them?

JOHN Yeah.

ICHABOD Oh yes.

JOHN You know that?

ICHABOD We know.

DYLAN Of course we know *that*. It's the *bane* of our fucking existence,
sweetheart. I mean it works for us and against us. At some parties it's
a turn on, at others, it's like the kiss of death. Jesus, it's not as if we
bareback. Even though we do. But we don't go around *talking* about
barebacking all the time, like some icky people. Have you ever met
a serious bugchaser? What crashing bores they are, and some of
them call themselves AIDS radicals. Pardon me while I puke—

ICHABOD Shut up.

DYLAN Yes, darling.

ICHABOD So, what.

JOHN *(looking at him, scared)* What.

ICHABOD You want to know? *(pause)*

JOHN Yes, I want to know. *(pause)*

ICHABOD Did we or didn't we?

JOHN I know. I feel like such a starfucker but *(He takes off one of his
shoes.)* it's turning me on. *(He puts the shoe on the floor, pointedly
away from him.)*

DYLAN Oh, honey, we like starfuckers. We like any kind of fuckers actually, especially when they look like you.

ICHABOD And so what if I told you, yes.

JOHN (*hangs his head, wipes his face with excitement*) Oh, God.

ICHABOD And now I suppose you want to know how.

JOHN (*taking off his other shoe*) Yeah. (*pause*)

ICHABOD With a bat. Or two bats I should say. Dylan had one and so did I.

JOHN You beat them to death?

ICHABOD In the head.

JOHN Oh fuck.

> *ICHABOD nods to DYLAN. DYLAN turns on some music, which has a very low, throbbing beat. He also dims the lights. DYLAN starts to dance, slowly, hypnotically. JOHN starts to take off his pants.*

ICHABOD We started with my sister.

JOHN Jesus, your fucking sister.

ICHABOD Yes, my sister. But she was such a deadhead already. She wouldn't die. So we left her for awhile, walking around and moaning.

JOHN (*stepping out of his pants*) And did you do your father next?

ICHABOD Dylan was already working on my father. He was easy, a couple of swings.

DYLAN (*swaying to the music*) Swings...

ICHABOD And he was done.

JOHN Oh... fuck.

ICHABOD My mother was already screaming, of course.

JOHN Screaming. (*He does a kind of strip tease in his underwear, slowly pulling it off.*)

ICHABOD So while Dylan went back and finished my sister...

JOHN (*stepping out of his underpants*) Jesus... Jesus... Jesus...

ICHABOD I did my mother. She was a hard one. A hard head. She screamed for awhile. But I kept saying over and over again—"what are you screaming for, Mother... you're already dead..."

DYLAN Already dead...

JOHN *(starts to do a stripper dance, naked)* Jesus you guys...

ICHABOD So... that's how it all happened...

> *There is a pause, for a moment. ICHABOD claps his hands. ICHABOD comes out of his trance and goes behind JOHN and starts to eat his ass. DYLAN goes around the front of him and starts to suck his cock. They do this for a few seconds, then—*

DYLAN I knew he was a starfucker.

ICHABOD Shut up.

> *They continue doing their work. The lights dim to black. Pause. The music swells and continues in the dark. Lights up on CECILIA's lovely chair, and there is another matching one opposite hers. A table beside it, with coffee. BOBBI sits in it.*

CECILIA That's strange, you drinking coffee.

BOBBI I always drink coffee.

CECILIA Not with me, with me, you drink tea.

BOBBI Oh, do I? I didn't notice. *(pause)* Is that significant?

CECILIA You tell me.

BOBBI Aren't we enigmatic.

CECILIA Yes, I'm feeling very enigmatic today. But not half as enigmatic as you.

BOBBI What are you talking about?

CECILIA You have a hangover, don't you?

BOBBI Well maybe I do. Is that a crime?

CECILIA No of course not. It's not a crime. It's just... you know I worry about you.

BOBBI Don't bother.

CECILIA I can't help it. It's the mother in me. It comes from not having any children.

BOBBI You hate children.

CECILIA Yes, I know I do, but the need still throbs in me. It does in any woman. Like a phantom limb.

BOBBI That's an essentialist notion.

CECILIA Well aren't we intelligent today.

BOBBI I'm intelligent every day.

CECILIA Which is why I love you so dearly.

BOBBI No really. I know several stone butch lesbians who don't have the need, anywhere, to have children. Never did, never will.

CECILIA Well I'm not a stone butch lesbian—

BOBBI Thank God—

CECILIA Thank God—

BOBBI Don't tell anybody I said that.

CECILIA Why on earth not?

BOBBI Now that I'm the chairman of The Rainbow Channel I'm not allowed to say anything nasty about anyone anymore.

CECILIA I see.

BOBBI Especially stone butch lesbians. *(pause)* And transgenders.

CECILIA What are transgenders exactly?

BOBBI I'm never sure. Perpetually hurt and left out people as far as I can tell. And don't tell anyone I said that either.

CECILIA You know our little *tête-á-têtes* are not for publication.

BOBBI Everything else is.

CECILIA Absolutely everything yes. *(pause)* So did you and Rod go out last night?

BOBBI Yes we did.

CECILIA Did you have what people euphemistically call, fun?

BOBBI We had quite a lot of fun.

CECILIA I'm convinced it's just jealousy.

BOBBI What?

CECILIA Some day I'm going to write a column about it. It's why heterosexuals hate you so much. Because you're having so much more fun than we are.

BOBBI Not necessarily.

CECILIA No, you are, you definitely are.

BOBBI But you and Lance still get it on, occasionally, don't you?

CECILIA Yes.

BOBBI I would think he'd be very virile in a bear-like way.

CECILIA I'm not telling you any details.

BOBBI Too bad.

CECILIA But bear-like is not far off.

BOBBI One for me.

CECILIA So you and Roddi met someone?

BOBBI You are *prying* today. What's this all about?

CECILIA Well this whole open relationship thing. I don't understand.

BOBBI I'm not too sure I understand it either.

CECILIA It was Roddi's idea, wasn't it?

BOBBI Stop calling him Roddi. His name is Rod.

CECILIA He's always seemed like a Roddi to me. Roddi and Bobbi. It's all so...

BOBBI Gay?

CECILIA I didn't want to say it.

BOBBI Yes you did. *(pause)* What are you getting at with all this?

CECILIA Well I just think the whole idea of you two going out and finding people together was sort of his idea wasn't it?

BOBBI It was *our* idea.

CECILIA Oh, I see.

BOBBI What.

CECILIA Don't be defensive.

BOBBI I'm not. I told you already, but you don't believe me. We did it to save our relationship. We both had issues around promiscuity, but this isn't really promiscuity, because we do it together.

CECILIA If I told Lance about this he would laugh and laugh.

BOBBI Please don't tell him, he's homophobic enough already.

CECILIA I don't know if that's really true.

BOBBI Yes it is.

CECILIA I suppose you're right.

BOBBI Anyway, I resent you intimating that Rod is a bad influence. It's what you're suggesting isn't it?

CECILIA I'm not suggesting anything. I worry about you.

BOBBI Well it's very sweet.

CECILIA I know. I enjoy being a girl.

BOBBI But what's all this about, really.

CECILIA Why does it have to be about something?

BOBBI I'm sure this isn't just a catch up and gossip. You've got something up your sleeve.

CECILIA Have I?

BOBBI I'm sure you have.

CECILIA Little ol' me?

BOBBI Yes.

CECILIA Well maybe I have. *(Pause, she sets down her cup.)* I've got a great idea for an interview.

BOBBI I knew it.

CECILIA What.

BOBBI I hope it's not who I think it is.

CECILIA What's the problem?

BOBBI Not those two.

CECILIA Dylan Short and Ichabod Malframe.

BOBBI Cecilia, no.

CECILIA Why not? I don't understand. The police just arrested them. And the officer who secured their confession is a personal friend of mine.

BOBBI *(stands up)* I'll leave.

CECILIA Don't be ridiculous.

BOBBI I'm not being ridiculous.

CECILIA What's the problem?

BOBBI You know, sometimes you straight people—

CECILIA I really don't like it when you take that tone with me.

BOBBI And normally you don't act like one.

CECILIA What's so awful about interviewing them?

BOBBI If you don't know—

CECILIA Well you certainly have to tell me, how else am I going to figure it out.

BOBBI The reason I get so upset, is because it's elementary politics 101, but I suppose you can't really understand unless you're inside the culture.

CECILIA Don't condescend to me.

BOBBI I'm not. There's no way you could know, I suppose. *(He sits down.)* I want you to think very carefully, for a minute, about oppression, and homophobia, and the way gay men have been treated since time immemorial.

CECILIA I'm thinking.

BOBBI And then I want you to think about what these two guys have been accused of.

CECILIA The most heinous of crimes. Matricide. Parricide.

BOBBI How long ago was it that people thought all fags were evil? That all gay men were into molesting children? That they shouldn't be married, they should be ostracized from their families? And here we have two guys who have plotted to kill the one guy's parents, with baseball bats, no less, and on top of everything they just seem so fucking arrogant about it.

CECILIA But Bobbi. Look at me.

BOBBI What.

CECILIA *(She leans in.)* It's such a *great story*.

BOBBI Fuck Cecilia.

CECILIA What.

BOBBI Is that all that matters?

CECILIA Well, frankly, yes. *(pause)*

BOBBI Do you know what that's going to do to our community if they are convicted?

CECILIA Listen, Bobbi—

BOBBI It'll set us back years. No. *Centuries.* And no, I won't listen.

CECILIA Yes you will.

BOBBI No.

CECILIA *(reaching over and taking his hand)* Can I tell you something?

BOBBI *(annoyed)* What.

CECILIA This is really very important.

BOBBI What is it?

CECILIA I want you to think about this now, with all your fervour, with all your might, because I meant it today, as I always do, when I told you how intelligent you are. This is the situation. I am a cliché. I am nearly fifty years old, and I've been married to the same man for nearly thirty years. Obviously it's not the first careless rapture, is it? And my husband is, to say the least, married to his work, which now happens to be mainly concerned with keeping himself out of jail. And yet when I see a TV program or a movie, or read a novel about a neglected, rapidly aging forty-five-year-old housewife who is trapped in a loveless marriage with a husband who is cheating on her, I don't call up the TV station or call the publisher and complain that this is casting a disparaging light on my own personal demographic.

BOBBI That's not the same—

CECILIA And do you know why? Do you?

BOBBI *(sighing)* No—

CECILIA Because *that's not me*. I happen to be rapidly aging and over forty-five but there the resemblance ends. I am happy in my marriage to this man who neglects me somewhat because I'm so fucking busy and I love my career so much that with him I get the time to myself I need. And on top of that I happen to love him. So I'm not threatened. I'm not the least bit threatened. Oh, yes when I see one of those movies I'm annoyed. I see it and think there's another stupid cliché. But I am not driven to denounce it, I do not start to quiver with anger because that sad woman in the movie is not me. And she never will be.

BOBBI *(after a pause)* What are you saying?

CECILIA I'm merely suggesting—

BOBBI That I murdered my parents?

CECILIA No, no, you obviously haven't murdered your parents. I'm just suggesting you wouldn't be so deeply upset about this couple, or me interviewing this couple—which would be a major story for your TV station by the way, just from *your* reaction I can see it would up gay ratings one hundred percent, which your station desperately needs at the present moment—

BOBBI I'm aware of all that. I want to know exactly what you're suggesting.

CECILIA I'm suggesting, that the reason you're so upset about this is because there's something you're guilty of, something you're not telling me. Obviously I don't think you've killed anyone but there must be a lie you're holding on to, that's the only possible explanation. If there wasn't an aspect of this couple *in* you, something about them that reminds them of yourself, you wouldn't be so upset about them. I think there's some hypocrisy going on here, and if you're honest with yourself, you'll admit it. *(pause)* I'm just concerned about you, that's all.

BOBBI Are you concerned about me, or are you using emotional manipulation to try and get me to run your story?

CECILIA I'll admit I'm not above doing both at the same time. But my concern for you is truly sincere.

BOBBI I don't think so. *(He gets up.)* You know I've always enjoyed your company, Cecilia, our little teas and the verbal sparring that goes along with them. Of course it's been lots of fun to be friends with you, and get invited to your society parties and trade gossip and quips. But today I've seen a side of you that people have warned me about, but I never chose to believe was there.

CECILIA And what side is that?

BOBBI Naked ambition.

CECILIA How melodramatic.

BOBBI How sad that what is melodramatic is so often true. Goodbye Cecilia. I don't know if I'll ever have occasion to call you again.

CECILIA *(honestly)* I'm sorry, Bobbi.

BOBBI Are you? Or are you just mad you lost the story.

CECILIA I'm not mad. And I can sell this story anywhere. I just wanted to give you first crack at it.

BOBBI How can you be so stupid and insensitive. HAVE YOU LISTENED TO A WORD I'VE SAID? I don't want your STUPID STORY!

CECILIA Whatever you say.

BOBBI Goodbye. *(He goes to the door.)*

CECILIA Bobbi.

BOBBI I said goodbye.

CECILIA The one who gets mad is always hiding something.

BOBBI Fuck you. *(He exits. Pause. CECILIA sits down again.)*

> *A white room with three institutional chairs. It's a prison meeting room. DYLAN is at the window. ICHABOD is sitting in one of the chairs. ICHABOD appears to be very calm. DYLAN is antsy.*

DYLAN I thought there would be someone cute. *(pause)* It makes it very difficult that there's no one who's cute. *(pause)* Aren't you going to talk to me?

ICHABOD Black you mean.

DYLAN I don't mean black.

ICHABOD Yes you do.

DYLAN Why are you being so mean to me?

ICHABOD I'm always mean to you.

DYLAN But we're in prison. I haven't seen you in a month.

ICHABOD So does that mean I have to be nice to you all of a sudden?

DYLAN I love you. *(He kisses ICHABOD on the neck. ICHABOD doesn't respond.)* There's one white guy who has a gorgeous body.

ICHABOD But he's not your black prison fantasy.

DYLAN Yes.

ICHABOD You're a sexual racist.

DYLAN So how many Asian guys have you slept with in your lifetime, Mr. Racially Colourblind Sexual Democrat.

ICHABOD Hundreds.

DYLAN Oh. I'm *so* jealous. *(Pause, DYLAN wanders around the room.)* What do you know about this dumb lady?

ICHABOD She'd better be smart. That's all I have to say, she'd better be fucking smart.

DYLAN *(Pause, he wanders around the room.)* Don't you ever get scared?

ICHABOD No. What's there to be scared of? We didn't do it.

DYLAN We didn't?

ICHABOD *(annoyed)* No. *(pause)* Have you forgotten already?

DYLAN No. *(pause)* But lots of not-guilty people get the death penalty all the time. I saw it on "City Confidential."

ICHABOD And what does Judge Judy say?

DYLAN Judge Judy doesn't try murderers. *(pause)* Come on, aren't you a little bit horny?

ICHABOD Who says I'm not getting laid.

DYLAN Are you?

ICHABOD I don't have to tell you. We're not married.

DYLAN I know. I like that. *(pause)* Boy, if we got laid before, when we get out, we're *really* going to get laid. Imagine what starfuckers we'll get now.

ICHABOD The mind boggles.

DYLAN What?

ICHABOD I said the mind boggles.

> *ICHABOD seems to notice DYLAN for the first time, manages a thin little smile. The door opens. CECILIA walks in, a bit uncertainly. She carries a tape recorder.*

CECILIA Oh, hello.

DYLAN Hi. *(ICHABOD says nothing.)*

CECILIA I'm surprised they let me meet with you on my own, without some sort of escort. But this does seem like a nicer part of the jail.

DYLAN It is nicer.

CECILIA It's a bit more country clubbish.

DYLAN It's a jail for extra *special* people. It's called protective custody.

CECILIA They took me past your cells, and they've let you decorate them quite nicely.

DYLAN We had to bribe a lot of people, but it was completely worth it.

CECILIA I see. You both come from quite a bit of money, don't you?

DYLAN Yup.

CECILIA I'm sorry, I shouldn't just start asking questions without introducing myself. Besides my tape recorder isn't even on. Hello, I'm Cecilia Wainscott. Do you mind if I sit down?

DYLAN *(shrugs)* Sure.

CECILIA *(sits down and starts her recorder)* And you must be—

DYLAN I'm Dylan.

CECILIA I see. And you must be… *(ICHABOD stares at her.)*

DYLAN That's Ichabod. But he's acting weird today.

CECILIA Well I imagine jail, even if it is like a country club, could make anyone feel a little weird.

DYLAN I thought it would be a lot sexier.

CECILIA Prison?

DYLAN Yes.

CECILIA Well that's what you hear, if you believe "Oz." All my gay friends love that show. Almost as much as "Queer Eye for the Straight Guy."

> *Very suddenly and brutally, ICHABOD pushes his chair out from under him, with a loud noise. He walks towards the window. They turn and look at him, then DYLAN calmly turns back.*

DYLAN I can't watch "Oz" because I'm *never* home on Friday nights.

CECILIA Friday night is party night?

DYLAN Every night is party night.

CECILIA I must say that's an idea I've always understood. I think that's one of the thousands of things that makes me feel so close to my gay friends. Take for instance, New Years. My husband and I never observe it. As far as I can tell, it's simply an excuse to get roaring drunk. I don't need an excuse, and neither does my husband. All I can think of, is how depressing that these people only give themselves permission to let loose one night a year.

DYLAN *(pause)* Are you a fag hag? *(pause)* Look, Ichabod, they sent us a faghag. *(ICHABOD doesn't answer.)* I apologize for my hunnybunny. As I said he's a little weird today.

CECILIA That's alright. *(She clears her throat.)* Not that I'm necessarily, offended by the term faghag. Some of my best friends are faghags. But my understanding is that faghags actually sleep with homosexuals. I don't actually do that.

DYLAN Oh. I didn't think you did.

CECILIA Not that I have anything against that.

DYLAN I wouldn't care if you're a faghag. It just seems that you know a lot about fags.

CECILIA Yes, I suppose I do. *(pause)* I can't help being disconcerted by your friend's silence.

DYLAN Like I said, don't take it personally. He likes me to talk to people first. I'm the canary he sends into the coal mine.

CECILIA I see. *(Pause, she opens up her pad.)* So, Dylan, you're a native Torontonian.

DYLAN Yup.

CECILIA But Ichabod, I understand, is not.

DYLAN No, he's from Rochester. But he and his parents moved here when he was a kid.

CECILIA Ahh.

DYLAN I met him at a fuck party.

CECILIA I see.

DYLAN It was a fisting party.

CECILIA Ahh.

DYLAN I bet you've never been to a fisting party.

CECILIA I can't say that I have.

DYLAN Anyway, he was a student at the University of Toronto—

CECILIA Yes, I read that.

DYLAN But I got him to give up his studies.

CECILIA Yes?

DYLAN For me. And for the world. It's us and the world *act*ually. We've fucked half of it. When we get out we're going to fuck the other half.

CECILIA So you're certain you'll get out?

DYLAN One hundred percent. We're innocent.

CECILIA And yet you, or rather it was Ichabod, I think, confessed to the murder of his family.

DYLAN That was under duress.

CECILIA Under duress?

DYLAN Under duress of undressing. Under the duress of a cute boy undressing. You see, the cop told us that he would fuck us if we had killed Ichabod's parents. And when we started talking, he started stripping. It was all just part of a fuck scene really. That's what we're going to use in our defense. That we were entrapped. But the fuck scene was very good. It was actually completely worth it.

CECILIA He's a very cute cop. I know him.

DYLAN You do?

CECILIA Yes, he's a friend of mine.

DYLAN Is he gay?

CECILIA Well he's... undecided. His work, as you can imagine, gets him into a lot of sexual situations.

DYLAN Gee, I'd really like to fuck that guy again. He was absolutely adorable.

CECILIA Yes, he really is. *(She looks around, then leans in to DYLAN confidentially.)* I must admit I'm a bit disconcerted by your friend here.

DYLAN He's not my friend. He's my boyfriend. We fuck people together. That makes us boyfriends.

CECILIA Well, he's giving me the willies.

ICHABOD Don't talk about me as if I'm not here.

CECILIA I'm very sorry, but you weren't talking.

ICHABOD And that was your plan, to get me talking.

CECILIA I don't have a plan.

ICHABOD You don't?

CECILIA No I don't, honestly.

ICHABOD Right. *(pause)* I find you detestable.

CECILIA Ahh. That's too bad.

ICHABOD You're the kind of woman I hate. A rich, tightassed liberal fembot with a lot of trendy homosexual friends.

CECILIA Well I'd say you've got me pinned, so to speak, but that's not entirely correct. I'm a social liberal, but a fiscal conservative.

ICHABOD Like John Maynard Keynes?

CECILIA I don't think he was a fiscal conservative.

ICHABOD He didn't seem so at the time, but history has proved him to be the prophet of American socialism.

CECILIA At least you recognize that the American system is socialism.

ICHABOD Of course I do. I'm not stupid.

CECILIA What were you studying at the University of Toronto?

ICHABOD Philosophy. But I don't want to answer your stupid questions. You're a tightassed bitch who never gets laid.

CECILIA On the contrary, I do.

ICHABOD Say it, then.

CECILIA Say what.

ICHABOD Say the words. I get fucked.

CECILIA I get fucked.

ICHABOD You're still tightassed.

CECILIA Your standards are very high.

ICHABOD You're not kidding.

CECILIA So, are you looking forward to your acquittal?

ICHABOD I'm not so sure we'll be acquitted.

DYLAN But you said—

ICHABOD Shut up. *(pause)*

CECILIA You're not very nice to your friend.

ICHABOD That's another thing that drives me crazy about you people. No matter how many fucking homosexuals you claim to know and like you just can't get your mind around our relationships. Your language betrays you. And language, as you well know I'm sure, is all important. in fact, it's the most important thing in the world. You insist on calling him my friend when he's not. He's my boyfriend. We fuck each other and other people together. If you call him my friend one more time I'm going to puke. You don't know anything about my relationship and therefore you shouldn't make any attempt to judge it. I've got nothing to say about your husband but as I understand it he's fat and fifty and defending himself against fraud charges as we speak. Oh that must just be a perfect little relationship. How is your *friend* Lance DeWitt? Do you call your husband your *friend*?

CECILIA You seem to have somewhat of a chip on your shoulder, Mr. Malframe.

ICHABOD Oh do I? Do I? It's not a fucking chip it's a brick no it's a boulder. And it's not on my shoulder it's on my fucking back and it's crushing me. So listen to me little Miss Cozy With The Faggots Tits, you came for a story, so I'll give it to you, because I can tell you're not going to go away until you get it. Yes we did it, and there's news for you. And I'll tell you why we did it—

DYLAN *(standing)* But Ichabod—

ICHABOD *(savagely)* SHUT THE FUCK UP YOU IDIOT.

DYLAN *(stamping his feet, moving to the window)* Fuck!

ICHABOD I want you to think a little bit about what role models are out there in the world for us, as gay men. You mentioned one of them, didn't you? "Queer Eye for the Straight Guy," and then there's oh yes, there's "Will and Grace." Have you heard of that show, Ms Wainscott?

CECILIA Wainscott is my maiden name, which means I go by Miss.

ICHABOD Oh, I see, affirming your heterosexuality yet again, how comforting for you. Best policy when you're feeling threatened. Don't worry. All I have is words, words, words and as we both know, the pen isn't mightier than the sword, or is it Miss Wainscott? So have you seen those shows?

CECILIA Yes, I have.

ICHABOD And, did you like them?

CECILIA I have a feeling that whatever I say will be wrong.

ICHABOD Your tactfulness is getting increasingly rude. I asked you a question, do you like those TV shows?

CECILIA I haven't watched them in a while, but when they were on TV I did find them… mildly amusing.

ICHABOD I see, mildly amusing. Is that sort of like heh heh? *(He does a very minor laugh.)* Or more like hah hah? *(slightly broader)*

CECILIA More like heh heh.

ICHABOD I see. Well the images that you see on television, for television is, sadly, the apotheosis of our culture, are the images that we have to model ourselves upon. However banal or embarrassing television is, we must accept it as the measure of our culture, as the ultimate marker. We can claim to have mastered quantum physics, or poststructuralism, or have discovered that the universe is nothing more than a cocktail party, we can discover the pill for every disease in the world, including homosexuality, and yet we are still numbskulls who watch television. It is there we find images of who we are, it is our most telling form of verisimilitude. And what does television offer us? We have two choices as homosexual men, we can be unfunny closet cases who live with women and have no personal lives, like Will, on "Will and Grace," or we can be funny, effeminate inconsequential designers, decorators, and hairdressers who have an informed opinion on the next lamp or the right wine. Those are our choices. But do you notice something about those choices my dearest darling honey? Do you notice something about those precious role models we have before us sweetie pie?

CECILIA I'm sorry but I don't respond to honey or sweetie pie. I don't respond to misogyny.

ICHABOD I see. Well that's too bad. That's too fucking bad Miss Moneytits. I have no choice but to *respond* to homophobia. If I didn't respond every day, then I could go to the bank or take a fucking shit in a public washroom because it's all around me. But we'll leave that for now. Back to television. You see what those models offered us was sadly lacking in one thing, intelligence. Substance. The homosexuals you see all around you they can't reproduce, they are not biologically part of the cultural scheme of things so they ultimately don't matter. They are not important. But most of all, they are not intelligent. I think that's what irks us the most. Doesn't it Dylan?

DYLAN *(confused and lost)* Ichabod—

ICHABOD Yes it does. So Dylan and I did not choose that road. We chose another pair of role models. Two people who were not on television. Two people who appeared before television made homosexuals banal. We chose Leopold and Loeb.

CECILIA *(unable to contain her excitement)* Ahh.

ICHABOD Oh yes, Cecilia, yes, get that down, on your tape recorder and in print, that's very very important. There's one thing about Leopold and Loeb they are beautiful, and they are smart, and they are fucking, and they have real fun, and they have ideas, even though those ideas are somewhat fascistic. But as a fiscal conservative you must have a passing acquaintance with fascism.

CECILIA Well, I can't say that I—

ICHABOD No, you're probably a libertarian, or a Randian, yes I would think you are a Randian perhaps, at least from reading your columns you talk a lot about personal liberty, well here you have the ultimate in personal liberty, we murdered three people who were idiots, complete idiots. My father was just simply dumb, a dumb victim, he never hurt a flea but he wandered through life as a somnambulist or better yet a zombie, a night of the living dead and my mother, my mother was a sexual and emotional adolescent, it was "A Streetcar Named Desire" with her, she was always groping me YES MY MOTHER MADE ME A HOMOSEXUAL oh really can she make me one too? And my sister, well we won't even talk about her she was artistic, I mean autistic, did I say artistic? Well she was that too, an autistic modern artist, a primitive I think they called her a modern urban primitive, she painted stick figures and for a while she lived in the car and she exhibited at all the best galleries, so of course she had to be killed and that's the truth Miss Wainscott Miss socially liberal fiscal conservative ever so open-minded yes I do fuck Wainscott so put that in your faghag pipe and smoke it. *(pause)*

CECILIA I think I'm running out of tape. *(pause)* Yes, that's all. It's gone. I should have brought an extra.

ICHABOD That's not very professional. You didn't bring a spare? I'm surprised Miss Wainscott, truly surprised. Perhaps you've got lots of tapes in your car it's just that I've just intimidated the hell out of you so you have to get the fuck out.

CECILIA Perhaps I just need to collect my thoughts.

ICHABOD Well, I've intimidated you, I bet you're not intimidated by your much vaunted homosexual friends. Your little Wills and you play the Grace, and you talk about your Lance, and you compare their little sexual stories with yours, and that's oh so oh so liberal of you.

CECILIA I think I'll just pack up now.

ICHABOD I see. Do you find me too abusive? Can you say that I'm abusive, or are you too polite to say it?

CECILIA I can say it.

ICHABOD Then say it.

CECILIA Words are very important to you, aren't they?

ICHABOD Sometimes they are, and sometimes they aren't. In case you haven't noticed.

CECILIA I wonder why that is?

> *ICHABOD doesn't answer. CECILIA shrugs and begins to pack up.*

ICHABOD Well, thank you, it's been just lovely. I feel like I've poured my heart out to you, to you and the media. It's been lovely almost purging, even cathartic, I feel I have closure at last, ah, closure yes, finally, I can breathe now, ahh.

CECILIA It's been nice meeting you, Mr. Malframe.

ICHABOD No it hasn't.

CECILIA And you too, Mr. Short.

ICHABOD *(not turning around)* Thank you.

CECILIA *(She goes towards the door, stops, then turns back.)* Oh yes Dylan, I forgot to ask you, my readers might be interested in this, there is a rumour going around. Are you or aren't you related to Martin Short?

DYLAN *(after a pause, his back to her)* He's my second cousin.

CECILIA Ahh. Well that clears that up.

ICHABOD Good angle, good angle, Miss Wainscott, murderers, murderers with a connection to Hollywood Royalty, excellent, you can sell this story to "Hollywood Confidential" or better yet "Celebrity Justice," I imagine you'll get a pretty penny for it, or at least fame, which is what you're after, because with a husband like that, you're already filthy rich, or at least filthy.

CECILIA Good day, Mr. Malframe.

ICHABOD I'd say so.

> *CECILIA leaves. Pause, DYLAN stands with his back to*
> *ICHABOD for a few seconds.*

DYLAN I don't understand.

ICHABOD Oh just leave it to me. You're such an idiot. Just shut up and leave it to me.

DYLAN What's our lawyer going to do now.

ICHABOD Oh he's an idiot too. *(pause)*

DYLAN *(snivelling, turns around)* But I thought you said we didn't do it.

ICHABOD Oh Dylan, Dylan, my beautiful Dylan. *(He takes out a cigarette, lights it.)* Can't you see it doesn't matter?

DYLAN Why?

ICHABOD Let me explain, one more time. *(He stares at him.)*

> *The lights dim to black. A phone rings in the dark. Lights up on*
> *CECILIA on the phone.*

CECILIA Hello, Professor Stimowitz, this is Cecilia Wainscott. *(pause)* Yes, the famous—but no I don't like to think of myself that way. *(pause)* How nice of you to ask. My husband is fine. *(pause)* Well no, he's very resilient. *(pause)* So, as you might imagine, my journalistic research has led me into the unlikely realm of theoretical mathematics. *(pause)* Unlikely for me, perhaps, obviously not so for you. *(pause)* Well, I was wondering if you could give me some information about the Liar's Paradox. I understand that you are one of the world's leading experts. *(pause)* I see, that's logic, my mistake. *(pause)* But set theory and the liar's paradox are somehow inter-related? *(pause)* Ahh. *(pause)* Yes, laymen's terms are always helpful. Oh yes, a barber. Yes. *(A longer pause, then she begins to take notes.)* The set of all people who do not shave themselves. *(pause)* Well obviously that would be impossible, *(She laughs.)* hence the paradox, yes. And how long has this contradiction been a problem? *(pause)* From the dawn of time, lovely, I get your point, but in theoretical mathematics or rather logic... I see, about four hundred years. Now let me ask you a question, Professor Stimowitz, if someone were to write a paper in which they used inconsistent mathematics to solve the Liar's Paradox would that be a very important paper? *(pause)* Professor Stimowitz, are you alright?

(pause) I had no idea theoretical mathematicians could be so... passionate. *(pause)* I see, of course, it's your subject. Well no I don't have the paper. I may be able to get the paper for you, after a certain murder trial is over, if all goes according to plan. Yes. But I do want to thank you, you've been very helpful and— *(pause)* What? *(pause)* Yes, I'll do my best to get you access to that paper. Thank you so much. Goodbye.

> *She puts down the phone then impetuously picks it up and dials another number. Lights up on another telephone. BOBBI suddenly appears, around a corner. He appears to be just finishing dressing, in a rush. He looks at the call ID on the phone. Then, impetuously, he picks it up.*

BOBBI I thought I told you never to call me.

CECILIA You said you'd never call me.

BOBBI Cecilia, I'm serious.

CECILIA I know—

BOBBI Because if you think I'm not—

CECILIA No, I think you're serious. *(pause)* Why did you pick up the phone? I know you have call ID.

BOBBI I know you know I have call ID. *(pause)* Because I'm crazy in a rush and I wasn't thinking.

CECILIA You were thinking about how you always used to pick up the phone.

BOBBI It was just a habit.

CECILIA Was it?

BOBBI Look, Cecilia, this is a serious issue to me. You know how I feel about gay representation in the media. I'd start a gay anti-defamation league in Canada if I could. It's very important to me. It's not a small issue.

CECILIA I know. And that's why I wanted to say I'm sorry. I really am. I realized after I talked to you that it was unfair of me to accuse you like that.

BOBBI Well it certainly was but that isn't going to get you off the hook.

> *Pause.*

CECILIA I've talked to them.

BOBBI I'm not interested.

CECILIA Not even a little bit?

BOBBI No, I told you I'm not. *(Pause, he can't resist.)* The only possible thing I could possibly be interested in, if I were interested, because I'm not, is, are they cute?

CECILIA Oh Bobbi, I miss you.

BOBBI I've seen their pictures in the paper and they look as if they might be a pretty gorgeous couple, which makes a difference. Politically, I mean. I'm talking about public perception.

CECILIA You're very sweet. *(pause)* Yes, I think they're cute.

BOBBI Gay cute or straight cute?

CECILIA Oh come on, there's a universal cute.

BOBBI No there isn't.

CECILIA I think we're having fun again.

BOBBI Are we?

CECILIA You know we are. *(pause)* Actually, they look like a couple of hairdressers, very chic, very well groomed, saucy, very gay, you know the type. One of them is a hairdresser, actually, one of the best in the country it turns out. And the other—

BOBBI Ichabod—

CECILIA You are interested—

BOBBI He seems like the leader of the pack.

CECILIA Oh he is, he definitely is, and I've done some research and he's quite a fascinating character. I think he might even be a genius. I mean the Nobel prize-winning kind. In fact I'm sure he is.

BOBBI I'm not interested.

CECILIA I think you are.

BOBBI Cecilia, I have to get off. I shouldn't even have answered the phone.

CECILIA But you did.

BOBBI That doesn't mean anything.

CECILIA Yes it does. *(pause)* Bobbi—

BOBBI I have to go.

CECILIA But I just wanted to say, please don't cut me off, that the reason I was so severe with you yesterday was because I hear all these stories in the media, and I know it's the media, you and I, of all people, should know about the media, you hear about the worrying rise in unsafe sex among gay men. And I worry about you Bobbi, I have to admit I worry about you, and I think, when I accused you of hiding something, it was at the back of my mind.

BOBBI I see, so you really *don't* trust me.

CECILIA I didn't say that, maybe I was manipulated by the media, I don't know—but it came from a very sincere—

BOBBI Concern. For your information, my sex life is my business and I can take care of myself and I severely resent your patronizing tone. The fact that you would think I'm stupid enough to have unsafe sex in this day and age just proves that you have no right to call yourself my friend. Goodbye.

CECILIA I'm sure you're telling me the truth.

BOBBI Then what's the issue?

CECILIA It's just suddenly occurred to me—that if you were lying— how much power a liar has.

BOBBI Oh fuck off.

> *BOBBI slams down the phone. Lights up on JOHN, sitting in his room in the bathhouse, in a towel, steam around him, so that he's hard to see.*

JOHN I deal a lot with truth and lies. It's my job. And one thing I learn in my job is that, well, sometimes there's not a fine line. Like, for instance with those two homosexual killers. The ones that are on trial now. It doesn't look too good for them. And you could say that I was lying to them when I pretended that I was turned on by them so that I could turn them in. Well the way I look at it is like this. It's not lying if it's for a good cause. First of all, I was not lying about being attracted to them. Or maybe I should put it this way, it's pretty hard for a guy to lie about that sort of thing, and with me, well, I'm just in the lucky situation that—what turns me on is when, to be truthful here, really truthful, when somebody's attracted to me. This aspect of my character has proved pretty practical when it comes to well, my work. *(He adjusts his towel.)* And secondly, the most important thing is that what was a minor lie in this situation, the fact that I posed as some trick in order to trap them, well that was a small lie in order to serve the public good, and that's to put these crazy fuckers behind bars for life. The reason I can talk to you about this is because I've thought about it a lot. People are always accusing me of lying when it comes to, my sexual orientation. People are strange that way. They always want to pin you down. You have to be one or the other. Straight or gay. Jesus. Haven't you ever heard of bisexuals? What I try to make them understand that for me, it's possible to be homosexual for that one night, that one moment, forever, if it serves the greater good. And that's what I do. Serve the greater good. Do you get the picture? *(He looks out, waves away the steam.)* Can you even see me?

> *Rock bathhouse muzak plays. JOHN walks out of his room and is in a cruising space in a bathhouse. BOBBI is standing by a post, wearing a towel. JOHN stands opposite him. They look at each other for awhile. JOHN acts as if he is having trouble enduring BOBBI's flirtatious gaze. Finally he gives in and responds, looking down at him laughing.*

BOBBI Sorry.

JOHN It's okay.

BOBBI I couldn't help staring at you.

JOHN Hey, there's no one else here to stare at.

BOBBI That's what I like about it at this time of day.

JOHN Yeah?

BOBBI Yes.

JOHN *(after a pause)* You come here often?

BOBBI The truth?

JOHN The truth.

BOBBI *(laughing, embarrassed)* I'm very naughty. *(Pause, he looks at JOHN levelly.)* Yes. *(JOHN stares at him calmly and smiles.)* I've never told anyone that before.

JOHN Oh yeah.

BOBBI But you… got it out of me.

JOHN I have kind of a… knack, for getting the truth out of people.

BOBBI I can see that.

JOHN It's kinda… my job.

BOBBI Oh yeah?

JOHN Uh-huh.

BOBBI What are you, a human lie-detector?

JOHN Sort of.

BOBBI Hey, the body of death kinda helps.

JOHN I use it when I can.

BOBBI Are you using it now?

JOHN Well, it's just… there.

BOBBI I can see that. *(pause)* Work out much?

JOHN Well—

BOBBI Sorry. Just kidding. You obviously do. You know a guy like you wouldn't even look at me if this place wasn't empty.

JOHN Not true.

BOBBI No?

JOHN No. *(pause)*

BOBBI People like to say that the baths are democratic, but they're not. Everyone knows that.

JOHN Well no place in life is.

BOBBI True enough. *(pause)* I like it here though. *(pause)* I know you're not supposed to say that. You're supposed to say you hate it, and you never come here. But in *my* work… everybody kind of… knows me on the scene, I'm kind of a powerful person I guess, and well when you come here you know you're in different kind of space.

JOHN *(smiling)* You could say that.

BOBBI No I mean it. It's a fantasy place. Everyone's in towels and sort of floating around, and it's kind of like being in no place. It's very freeing, you sort of move around and bump into people, or not, plug in, or not, and nobody really cares who you are or what you do, or even what your political or religious category is, or even what your sexual orientation is. It's not that nobody's judging, everybody's judging your body, your pecs, your abs your… cock, but that's all they care about. It's an ideal world. Like living on a cloud.

JOHN I guess you could say that.

BOBBI No, it's true. Everybody looks the same, in a way. Except for you of course. Nobody looks like you. But nobody really has an identity, that is, you don't have to tell anybody your name. Or your real name, anyway. *(pause)* By the way, what *is* your name.

JOHN John. *(Pause. BOBBI smiles.)*

BOBBI Oh, come on.

JOHN No, really.

BOBBI Your name is John?

JOHN Yes, no kidding.

BOBBI I see. What's your last name.

JOHN Oh, now you're really gonna think I'm lying.

BOBBI Try me.

JOHN Believe me now. I'm telling you truth. I really am. It's… Trick.

BOBBI John… *Trick?*

JOHN *(laughing)* Yeah. Nobody ever believes me.

BOBBI In other words, your first name is the same as your last name. At least in gay lingo.

JOHN Sort of.

BOBBI Hmm. I find that very hard to believe.

JOHN Look at it this way. If I was gonna make up a name, would I use John Trick as a fake one? Who would believe it?

BOBBI Only someone stupid.

JOHN Yeah, but you're not stupid. *(pause)* Neither am I.

BOBBI No, you're not. *(Pause, they look at each other.)* I've got a room. *(pause)* Would you like to… come and visit?

JOHN *(after what seems like an interminable length of time)* Sure.

> *They slowly walk off together, into the dark. Lights dim to black. Up on ICHABOD and DYLAN. They are at the table, in the prison waiting room again, staring at the ringing telephone which is on the wall on the other side of the room.*

ICHABOD Do you want to get that? *(pause)*

DYLAN Do you think it's for us?

ICHABOD *(shrugs)* I don't know. *(He walks across the room and picks up the phone.)* Hello?

DYLAN *(whispers)* Who is it?

> *Pause, ICHABOD waves him away and listens. ICHABOD holds the phone away from his mouth, and looks straight ahead.*

Who is it?

ICHABOD It's my parents.

DYLAN *(incredulous)* Your parents?

ICHABOD Yes.

DYLAN How can it be your parents?

ICHABOD You want to speak to them?

DYLAN *(warily)* Okay. *(ICHABOD walks across the room to DYLAN. The phone has a cord on it, and the phone stretches across the room, it is a surrealistic image—a terribly long cord. He hands the phone to DYLAN.)* Hello? We're doing okay. Having some ups and downs. Why? *(pause)* Okay, thanks. *(pause)* Bye.

ICHABOD What did they have to say?

DYLAN They wanted to know how we're doing.

ICHABOD *(cheerily)* Oh.

DYLAN Ichabod.

ICHABOD Yes.

DYLAN Who were those people?

ICHABOD My parents.

DYLAN picks up the phone.

DYLAN Hello?

DYLAN looks at the phone and slowly puts it back on the receiver, staring at ICHABOD. The lights dim to black.

ACT TWO

Up on the prison room again. This time DYLAN is in a chair, his head in his hands, and ICHABOD is at the window.

ICHABOD *(after a pause)* I don't see what you're so upset about.

DYLAN I haven't seen you for a month. Except in court. The last time I saw you alone was the last time she came here. I haven't seen you at all. I love you. And then, on top of that you keep changing our story and now they they think we're crazy, and they're going to send us to an insane asylum for sure.

ICHABOD You don't know that.

DYLAN Our lawyer says that they don't have any evidence against us, but we're obviously crazy. At least you are.

ICHABOD He's stupid.

DYLAN I don't understand! *(He gets up.)* I don't understand why we're doing this! I don't know what this is all about any more. At first it was about getting laid. That's what it was *supposed* to be about. But now it's not about that at all. At least I haven't been laid in two months. I don't know about you.

ICHABOD It's best you don't think about that.

DYLAN Well I'm glad you're having a gay old time. What am I supposed to do?

ICHABOD Trust me.

DYLAN Trust you? Fuck Ichabod, how much trust is a person supposed to have?

ICHABOD *(turning away from the window)* Okay. Are you finished?

DYLAN Yes I'm finished. But you have to tell me what's going on now! Quick, before she comes. I can't stand this any more. I can't stand it I'm going crazy! Is that what you want? To drive me crazy? Is that what this is all about?

ICHABOD *(after a pause)* I said, are you finished?

DYLAN Yes, I'm finished.

ICHABOD Then shut up and listen. *(He sits down opposite DYLAN and takes his hands.)* Now I want you to think very carefully and use your brain, which is something that I know you're not used to doing. But just try. Just try and remain calm for a minute, and use your logic. I know you're a lot smarter than people think, or else I wouldn't be dating you. It's just that you never used half your brain power anyway, and you've destroyed the other half with E.

DYLAN Oh yeah, thanks—

ICHABOD Did I say you could talk? Now shut up, listen and think, that's all you have to do right now. I'm going to tell you what's going on. So the first big question is, do you still love me? *(pause)* Well? Well?

DYLAN You told me to shut up and think.

ICHABOD Not when I ask you a question, brainless. I asked you a question, so answer it.

DYLAN Yes, yes of course I love you.

ICHABOD Even after all we've gone through together.

DYLAN Yes I'll always love you, you know that.

ICHABOD Okay. So you know what love means? *(pause)* I asked you a question. Do you know what it means?

DYLAN *(after a pause)* Never having to say you're sorry?

ICHABOD No you numbskull, you have to say you're sorry all the time, especially if you're you and you don't think all the time and open your mouth and make thousands of mistakes and don't trust me. No, love means that you have to give up a few of your creature comforts for the person you love once in a while, because you love them and you want them to be happy.

DYLAN Creature comforts? Creature comforts? We're in fucking jail. It looks like the best we can hope for, if we're lucky and don't get the gas chamber or an insane asylum for life.

ICHABOD They don't have the gas chamber in Canada, Dylan.

DYLAN Oh great, that's really comforting, well that's one thing we don't have to worry about.

ICHABOD No, what you have to do, is trust me, because I know best. Ichabod knows best, right?

DYLAN *(somewhat mollified)* Yes, Ichabod knows best.

ICHABOD Ichabod knows best. Now I promise you, at the end of all this, at the end of it we're going to get everything you want. Little Dylan is going to get all the fucks he wants and all the drugs he wants, and life is going to be easy and he's never going to have to do a stick of work and he's going to be with his lover, me. Do you understand? But in the meantime, selfish, little impatient Dylan may just have to make one or two sacrifices because he loves Ichabod, and he trusts him and has agreed to give over his life into his care. I mean that's the big question, Dylan, and it's a pretty important one. Do you love me and trust me to support me in this or not?

DYLAN Well, you're asking a lot.

ICHABOD *(getting up)* Well great, then it's over, you and I are over and this, this whole fucking thing is over and you'll have to make it on your own.

DYLAN *(after a pause)* I don't want that.

ICHABOD I know that.

DYLAN I want you. I want to be with you again and be happy the way we were.

ICHABOD We will be, soon, I promise, just trust me.

DYLAN I do Ichabod.

ICHABOD Good. You'd better. You don't have any choice.

DYLAN I love you Ichabod.

ICHABOD I love you too, Dylan. *(They kiss.)*

DYLAN And it's going to be like it was before.

ICHABOD Yes, yes, I promise.

> There is a knock on the door, and then it tentatively opens.

CECILIA Hello? *(They break apart.)*

DYLAN *(wiping his eyes)* Hi.

> ICHABOD gets up and goes to the window again.

CECILIA I hope I'm not interrupting anything.

DYLAN No, it's okay, we're done.

CECILIA Dylan, have you been crying?

DYLAN No. *(He wipes his eyes furiously.)* Only a little bit.

CECILIA sits down opposite DYLAN and offers him some Kleenex.

CECILIA Here.

DYLAN Thank you.

CECILIA Have you and Ichabod been fighting?

DYLAN *(blowing his nose)* It's over now.

CECILIA Oh, that's good.

DYLAN We're just going through some... big life changes.

CECILIA I guess you are. *(pause)*

DYLAN Relationships... can be tough.

CECILIA *(knowingly)* Yes, I know they can. *(Pause, she comforts him.)* There, is that better?

DYLAN Yes.

ICHABOD has been watching them, annoyed.

ICHABOD Where's your tape recorder?

CECILIA I didn't bring it. I didn't come for an interview.

ICHABOD They told us you did.

CECILIA That was so you'd agree to see me. I'll be frank Ichabod, because I think it's the best route to take with you. Your lawyer wanted me to do what I could to persuade you to go on the witness stand.

ICHABOD I thought so. What a stupid nerd.

CECILIA Ichabod, sometimes I think you think everyone in the world is stupid.

ICHABOD But they are. *(Pause. She stands up.)*

CECILIA Well, the interview was a ruse this time. I came because I was concerned. *(Pause, she turns to ICHABOD, her voice is pointedly firm.)* Ichabod, what is your opinion of Brazilian logic?

> *ICHABOD, who has had his back turned to her, looks as if he has been hit—there is the subtlest but most significant motion of his shoulders.*

ICHABOD *(turning around, slowly, with a smile pasted on his face)* It can be pretty wacky.

CECILIA *(holding her own)* Oh, can it?

ICHABOD Yes, Dylan and I had a Brazilian once, with this thing or should I say wang?

DYLAN *(through with his sniffling)* You should say wang.

ICHABOD Yes, it was magnificent, and he wanted to put it up me. But I said no, no Mr. Brazilian from Brazil, you will not be putting that giant thang up me, up Dylan perhaps but not me.

DYLAN But I wouldn't let him either. I'm not crazy.

ICHABOD So we had to send him home. It was the waste of a wang. How much fun we could have had if he had only been willing to be sucked off. That's Brazilian logic for you, isn't it Dylan.

DYLAN *(recovering from his tears)* It was too big even for us. That's funny.

ICHABOD And that's Brazilian logic.

CECILIA You know what I'm talking about.

ICHABOD I don't think I do.

CECILIA In 1996 you wrote a landmark essay in which you refuted Bertrand Russell, Zermelo, Goedel and many others, and attempted, quite successfully I might add, to prove Mortenson's theory of inconsistent calculus.

ICHABOD It was a stupid essay.

CECILIA What was wrong with it?

ICHABOD It was inconsistent.

CECILIA Is that why you withdrew it from publication?

ICHABOD It's none of your business.

CECILIA It's the first instance I've ever heard of where an academic has produced a piece of scholarship that might have rocked the academic world, perhaps made history, and as your supervisor told me, even won the Nobel prize—and then removed the same work in the middle of publication.

ICHABOD I got bored with the inconsistency of it all. It was making me horny and I wanted to have sex.

CECILIA I see. You too, Dylan, have hidden your light under a bushel, though it might be seen as somewhat of a less penetrating one.

DYLAN What does she mean?

CECILIA Were you not the most sought after hairdresser at Damon Pythias Designs in Toronto—a world renowned hairdressing salon, until you quit, around the same time as Ichabod removed his earthshaking essay on theoretical mathematics?

ICHABOD So, this *is* an interview.

CECILIA In a way, everything is an interview. Life is an interview. I know you don't like to believe me when I say this Ichabod, but I'm actually concerned about you two. I mean after I've watched what's been happening in court and after doing a little research, I've come to a conclusion. You are a very disturbed young man, Ichabod Malframe, and I think you need someone's help.

ICHABOD You mean everyone's pity.

CECILIA That too.

ICHABOD Well I don't want it.

CECILIA You're going to get it from me anyway. I can't help it. *(She sits down, and opens up her purse.)* Now, I want to tell you a little bit more about the research I've done.

ICHABOD Not very professional of you not to have done it in the first place. I might just call the right wing journalists association and complain.

CECILIA There is no right wing journalists association and if there was I wouldn't belong to it. You were right before. I'm a libertarian, not a Randian, but a libertarian. And besides, I'm not speaking to just you this time Ichabod, it seems that you have a knack of making things all about you. It's a very special talent, in fact. Along with all the others which you so obviously have. Indeed, you are quite, quite gifted. But we'll leave that now, because you don't seem to want to talk about it. I have analyzed some of the information you've given the police and myself about the murders, and I would like to present my findings to you.

ICHABOD Oh, well bully for you. I'm so excited.

CECILIA I knew you would be. *(She unrolls a paper.)* Now it has become clear to me from testimony at the trial, clear to me and everyone else, Ichabod, that you have a very disarming habit of changing your story, and it is more and more obvious that the things which you say are simply that, stories, and the big question seems to be, why. Now the first story that you told, to the attractive and obviously persuasive young investigator, John Trick, was that you had killed your mother and father and autistic sister with a bat. You said that, and I quote, "And my mother and father… well they don't even bear talking about. There's *nothing* to talk about. Except how much I hated them. It was a fucking relief to get rid of them. Honestly. My mother… can I tell you how stupid she was? What a fucking victim? And my father molested me. He was a fucking faggot." Do you remember saying that?

ICHABOD You know what amazes me is that the lovely and prodigious John Trick, what an incredibly apt last name, was bugged. Where could he put it? I know it wasn't up his asshole because I was licking that, very thoroughly.

CECILIA *(undaunted)* They have remarkable ways of bugging people nowadays. Technology has made huge advances.

ICHABOD Those eggheady little Japs.

CECILIA Yes well, all racism aside, we know exactly what you said. And then you said to me, in our interview, and I quote "My father was just simply dumb, a dumb victim, he never hurt a flea but he wandered through life as a somnambulist or better yet a zombie, a night of the living dead and my mother, my mother was a sexual and emotional adolescent, it was "A Streetcar Named Desire" with her, she was always groping me YES MY MOTHER MADE ME A HOMOSEXUAL oh really can she make me one too?" So now we have two testimonies coming from you, two testimonies which are directly in conflict. In the first one, you said that your mother was the dumb one, and your father had molested you, and in the second you indicated that your father was a cipher and your mother molested you, now which is it?

ICHABOD They were both dumb molesting ciphers. I got mixed up. Can't a person get mixed up now and then? I'm not *perfect*! Everybody always expects me to be perfect. It's infuriating. I'll admit I'm pretty damn wonderful, but I'm not perfect, and that's the truth. I guess that's why you want them to put me on the witness stand so they can confront me with all these dazzling little empirical contradictions and I'll just break down weeping like the last five minutes of "Law and Order."

CECILIA You don't have to do that.

ICHABOD That's what my stupid lawyer wants.

CECILIA You should let him do it. If you went on the witness stand they'd see you are disturbed and you need help.

ICHABOD I'm not disturbed and I don't need help. You're the crazy one. The world is crazy. I'm fine. I see things very clearly. All there is to see, that is. Anyway, what about my dead autistic sister? I was consistent about her, wasn't I? If it's consistency you want. I don't see why it matters so much anyway.

CECILIA You also told me and I quote... oh I won't bother to quote, you told me that she was not autistic, but artistic.

ICHABOD Well you should have a look at your notes because I said she was artistic *and* autistic.

CECILIA Your sister was not an artist.

ICHABOD Yes she was.

CECILIA She was completely uncommunicative. She could barely eat and sleep.

ICHABOD She used to paint.

CECILIA There's no evidence of that.

ICHABOD I SAW HER PAINT! *(pause)* It wasn't very good of course. Stick figures like some little retarded kid would draw. Of course I've seen stuff like that sell for good money though.

CECILIA Really, Ichabod, it's hopeless, you are quite simply a liar, but the question is.... Why are you a liar? What has driven you to do this? Is it perhaps the murder of your parents that has traumatized you into lying? A murder which you didn't commit? Well I would imagine it would unhinge anyone to have their whole family murdered, and maybe the best way to deal with it would be to reject the notion that you ever loved them in the first place. What? No reaction? Well you're a very good actor Ichabod, so I don't trust your reactions anymore. We both know that your parents were far from dumb, and I doubt either of them molested you either. They were quite prominent professors at the University of Toronto, in fact you come from quite a gifted family.

ICHABOD Yeah yeah, well who cares.

CECILIA I care, and you should too. And so should Dylan. Dylan, do you care?

DYLAN *(eying ICHABOD out of the corner of his eye)* Sort of.

CECILIA Well you should. *(pause)* So, what do you have to say, Ichabod, now that I confront you with all this?

ICHABOD I don't have anything to say. *(pause)* What. I repent I repent I'm sorry I did it, I'm sorry?

CECILIA So you admit that you lied.

ICHABOD No, I don't. *(He pulls up a chair.)* Now let me ask you a question Miss Smartypants, who never bothered to do her research on the first interview, let me ask you this, because it happens to be very important and the key to everything, and I might as well tell you because I know now why you came here, you must be bugged too, my stupid lawyer is getting so desperate because I won't talk to him, and I won't and Dylan won't either ever, so you've probably got a bug up your asshole along with all that uptight white upperclass pseudo-fascist libertarian feminism and sexual frustration and a bunch of hemorrhoids. So since you're bugged and you want to know the truth so they can put us away in the crazy place with the rest of the crazies forever, I'll just give it to you. Now in all your research did you happen to discover what my parents my ever so intelligent parents were professors of? Because that happens to be very relevant, in case you want to know the key, what the key to all of this is.

CECILIA Yes, I did, in fact, discover that.

ICHABOD Okay, so, like, what.

CECILIA They were philosophy professors.

ICHABOD Yeah, right Elementary My Dear Watson they said that in court. But what were their dissertations on? What subjects were dear to their hearts? What did they teach? Or do you consider that irrelevant or is it just that you didn't do any research at all? Or are you and everybody else involved with this case just too stupid to understand what they taught and you're just repeating everything they said in court back to me and I'm getting very bored?

CECILIA *(calmly)* They were postmodernists.

ICHABOD Ahh, they were postmodernists. Did you hear that Dylan?

DYLAN I heard it.

ICHABOD Postmodernists. Now do you happen to know what postmodernism *is*? Miss Ms Wainscott Painscott Vainscott?

CECILIA *(stumbling a bit, looking at her notes)* Well it's a philosophy which… which… wait a minute I have some notes here, since you want me to be exact… and I know you do… which suggests that there is a… here… a self consciousness about the world about narrative, a self consciousness which can lead to a mixture, a pastiche of literary styles. There. Yes. That's my research.

ICHABOD Oh Cecilia, Cecilia, Cecilia. I think you know what Postmodernism is. Why are you pretending to be so stupid? Oh, just to make me talk. Well that's fine you see, you and I are a perfect match, because I love to talk. Now what you just gave me was a definition of literary postmodernism. That's very Linda Hutcheon and all but it's quite inept and not ultimately *relevant*. No, Miss Dumbypants who isn't even good at pretending she's stupid, they were philosophical postmodernists which is much more fundamental and is where all that literary postmodernism comes from. Now the philosophy of postmodernism, if you had bothered to do your reading, Miss Stupid, is a philosophy which suggests that in fact there is no certainty. There is no map of the world. There is no there there. It is not a philosophy which suggests that the world is hard to discover, or that, like Plato, it exists somewhere else and we are viewing only shadows on the wall, it insists instead that there is nothing, no plan, no scheme no truth, in fact *no certainty*. Everything is—to coin an Einsteinism, because it's all connected really, the whole twentieth century is connected—*relative*. And a corollary of that philosophy, is that there is no such thing as identity. Identity is an illusion, as is gender, ethnicity, race and sexual orientation. We all made these things up with language, and we are trapped in that. And so, ergo, in conclusion, I am not a homosexual, and neither is Dylan, and neither is anyone we fucked because we have no *identity* because there is no such thing as *homosexuality or gay*. Now I want you to imagine, for a minute, what it would be like to have parents who do not, I repeat, do not recoil in horror when you tell them you are gay, and do not live in denial and do not quote the Bible at you but simply relax, light a cigarette, laugh and tell you your identity is an *illusion*. I killed my parents because they were postmodernists and they denied my existence and Dylan's existence and millions of others and said we were all figments of *language*. And that was dumb, and that was abuse, and that's why I killed them, and that's why I was telling the truth. There. Are you satisfied now?

CECILIA *(staring at him, with wonder)* You are amazing. You are absolutely amazing. Well. Now I am convinced of it. I'm convinced of my diagnosis, and I'm going to take this tape back to your lawyer, because yes, I am bugged, Mr. Malframe and I am going to tell him my diagnosis. You are what I suspected and what your lawyer suspected. You are a compulsory confessor. You would confess to a black lynching in Louisiana in 1963 or a heterosexual rape if the spirit moved you. God knows who killed your parents. Perhaps it was the trauma of their death that inspired this lying spree. But I submit that it is a kind of disease that you have—a compulsion to confess to crimes that you did not commit, Ichabod Malframe, and that is a very uncommon, but fully documented illness and that is what you have and why you need help.

ICHABOD Illness? You say I have an illness?

CECILIA Yes.

ICHABOD An overwhelming need to confess?

CECILIA Yes.

ICHABOD Have you ever read what Foucault said about Christianity and the last three hundred years?

CECILIA So everything comes back to Foucault?

ICHABOD Oh you wouldn't like him, because he was a smart faggot. Let me dumb my reference down to a medium you may have perused at random and I know it isn't books. Have you ever watched Oprah or any other talk show on television? I submit to you that if I am ill, then so is everyone else and what you call my illness is just a mass hysteria shared by the entire western world.

CECILIA Of course. Of course you would submit that, you're very eloquent and very smart, Ichabod.

ICHABOD I rest my case.

CECILIA And that may be your problem. You may be a little bit *too* smart.

ICHABOD Well at least I'm not an interior decorator.

CECILIA No, you're not.

ICHABOD Good, I'm glad you've seen the light.

CECILIA *(turning to DYLAN)* And what do you think of what was just said Dylan? What's your opinion.

DYLAN I think Ichabod is very smart. And I love him. And I trust him. And I always will.

CECILIA Well. *(She goes to the door.)* My work is done here.

ICHABOD I have one more thing to say to you.

CECILIA What?

ICHABOD You are a homophobe.

CECILIA Ichabod, that is one thing I'm not.

ICHABOD Well, be deluded then. About your marriage and your feelings about me. It suits you and makes you happy.

CECILIA Goodbye. Goodbye, Dylan.

ICHABOD Catch ya later, at the next bugging. *(She exits. There is a pause, ICHABOD stands watching her for a minute or two and then says:)* Wow.

DYLAN Wow?

ICHABOD Wow.

DYLAN What do you mean?

ICHABOD Everything is going according to plan. That is, if I had one.

DYLAN That's good. I guess.

> *The lights dim to black. Up on the bathhouse. BOBBI shuts the
> door. He and JOHN are alone in a tiny room with a bed. BOBBI
> sits on it.*

BOBBI Hey.

JOHN Hey.

BOBBI Here we are.

JOHN Yup.

BOBBI Sit.

JOHN Okay.

BOBBI *(after a pause)* Okay, so I want everything to be completely clear
and above board. I don't want any vagueness, any bullshit. If there's
one thing about me, I'm always honest. Always. With everyone. And
I like people to know where they are with me. What is and is not.

JOHN *(tentative)* Okay.

BOBBI Now when I meet a guy like you, a guy who is, well there's no
other way to put it, perfect in every way, when I meet a guy like that,
there's one thing that comes to my mind. The ultimate fantasy, you
might say. Now I don't want to lay anything heavy on you. I don't
want you to think I'm pressuring you. If anything I say here is too
much for you, or it offends you, then you can walk right out the
door. That's the great thing about the baths, you can just walk right
out the door.

JOHN Right.

BOBBI It's not a big deal. At least I don't think it is. And most other
fags don't think it is if they were honest, which is what I'm being.
But some people think it's a big deal. And that's the problem. So
I want to find out which kind of fag you are, whether it's a big
deal for you or not, and we'll act accordingly. So I have to ask you
a question and it's a big question, and I just want you to be honest,
so we know where we stand.

JOHN Sure.

BOBBI Okay. Here's the question. How do you feel about unsafe sex?

Lights dim on them to near blackness, but they continue talking. We just can't hear them and can barely see them. Lights up on CECILIA sitting in the same chair as as the beginning of the play, on the other side of the stage.

CECILIA So, that's my story. It may seem only tangentially to have involved Bobbi. But I think it actually involves him very much. Because contrary to what Bobbi thinks, and contrary to what Ichabod thinks, I may not be a gay man, but I'm not a homophobe. I don't know quite what to say to prove that to you. The most important thing which I will mention is the fact that I stood by those two, through thick and thin, and it was mainly thin. The truth is, that everyone believed they were guilty, even though there was never a shred of hard evidence to convict them. Why? Because each time the jury and the spectators gazed at them, they were reminded of every villainous gay, every evil effeminate fag, every murderous transvestite, and every salivating homosexual pedophile who in their nightmares they imagined might be lusting after their sons. And of course the boys' silliness, their arrogance, and their camp sense of humour completely worked against them. They were just so *gay*. Ichabod was right, in a way, no matter how smart he is, and he is very very smart, people insisted on seeing him as an interior decorator. Of the evilest kind. And if I hadn't gone in there twice, into the lions den, and tried to pull the truth out of him, honestly, then the two of them might be rotting in jail for life.

Lights up full on BOBBI and JOHN again, but they are still dimly viewed.

So yes I did a very bad thing to Bobbi, but only because I cared about him. I paid for John to go and do a little research. I know you might think I'm prying, that it's none of my business. Well doesn't love give you a right? Loving someone? No, I am not in love with Bobbi. I am not a faghag.

In the semi-dark, JOHN climbs on BOBBI and starts to fuck him.

But I do love him, and the only thing that worries me about him is this—it's not just that he's having unsafe sex, and not telling his lover, and putting both of their lives in danger, it's not just the fact of that betrayal, the possibility that he is slowly or quickly, who cares, committing suicide and killing his partner without his partner's consent. What I think is dangerous about Bobbi and what I worry about is the fact that he is a hypocrite, the fact that he is lying to himself. And that he has no knowledge no knowledge whatever in any part of his being that he is doing that. How can people lie to themselves? I know how they can lie to other people. But how can they lie to themselves? And maybe it's all mixed up with Ichabod and Dylan. With Leopold and Loeb. How can you tell the truth to yourself when most of the truths of your life would drive everyone, not just the Christian right, quite crazy? There's one consolation of course. John Trick, at least tells the truth. I know I can trust him. He's like a beacon of light in the darkness. I asked him of course, when Bobbi asked you to have safe sex, you said no, of course, didn't you? John promised me that as soon as he found out what I wanted him to find out, he got the hell out of there. I can say that I have at least one gay friend, ironically named John Trick, who I know will always tell me the truth.

> *Lights dim on BOBBI and JOHN, as BOBBI lets out a moan as JOHN fucks him.*

I think about them sometimes. The other two. Ichabod and Dylan. Apparently they are still together, in some sort of mental institution that specializes in drug rehabilitation. It turned out they had managed to smuggle pills into prison or buy them there somehow and were pretty high through most of the trial. Well I hope they're okay. And I'm going to visit them sometime, I will. Two more things. One new thing and one old thing I admit now, after all this, I admit that there are… some… this is very difficult for me to say because, I think it will all come tumbling down, if I let in a crack of light a bit of dampness… which is it? Both probably, the whole thing will crumble, melt, like the Wicked Witch of the West. The fact is that yes, my marriage isn't… perfect and yes, there are problems between myself and my husband. And sometimes I don't know if I… if I… if I am still… in love with him.

> *Pause.*

Just so you know that I'm not deluding myself. And finally, and once again—I am not a homophobe. That is one thing I do know. Contrary to what Ichabod said, in one of his countless demented ramblings, there are some things of which one *can* be… certain.

She puffs on her cigarette as the lights dim. Lights up on DYLAN in the rehabilitation centre of a mental institution. He is wearing a hospital gown with the back open and a very stylish jockstrap. He sits in an institutional chair watching TV. ICHABOD enters.

ICHABOD Are you happy now?

DYLAN They gave me Percodan this morning.

ICHABOD You like Percodan, don't you?

DYLAN I *love* it. *(pause)*

ICHABOD What about that new orderly.

DYLAN On my God, he's so hot.

ICHABOD You know they have to have muscles to work here and do all that heavy patient lifting. And since no white people will do the job, only black people, so you'll always have a supply of hunky black guys.

DYLAN Sometimes I think I could live here forever.

ICHABOD Well we might and we might… not.

DYLAN Don't tell me, I want it to be a surprise.

ICHABOD Oh, it will be.

DYLAN Who are you fucking by the way?

ICHABOD None of your business.

DYLAN Okay.

ICHABOD Actually, I am looking for a doctor who it might be fun to do, together. The thing I like about gay doctors, is they always have a stash of great drugs at home. *(There is a buzzer.)*

DYLAN Time for another dose! *(He runs off.)*

ICHABOD You have fun honey. *(He kisses him, as DYLAN runs off. ICHABOD clicks on the TV. He flicks the channel to Phil Donahue who is doing a classic, old interview with men who deliberately infect others with AIDS.)* Hey wait a minute. Haven't I seen this one before? *(Pause. He shrugs and settles back in his chair.)* Who cares.

He continues to watch it as the lights dim to black.

The end.

Sky Gilbert is a writer, director, and drag queen *extraordinaire*. He was co-founder and artistic director of Buddies in Bad Times Theatre (North America's largest gay and lesbian theatre) for 18 years. His hit plays include *The Dressing Gown, Drag Queens on Trial, Play Murder, The Emotionalists* and the Dora Mavor Moore Award-winning *The Whore's Revenge*. His first three novels: *Guilty* (1998), *St. Stephen's* (1999) and *I Am Kasper Klotz* (2001) were critically acclaimed. ECW Press published Sky's first collection of poetry *Digressions of a Naked Party Girl* in 1998, and his theatre memoir *Ejaculations from the Charm Factory* in 2000. His second book of collected poems *Temptations for a Juvenile Delinquent* was published by ECW in November 2003. He was recently the recipient of The Margo Bindhardt Award (from the Toronto Arts Foundation), The Silver Ticket Award (from the Toronto Alliance for the Performing Arts), and the ReLit Award (for his fourth novel *An English Gentleman*), and also recently received a PhD from the University of Toronto. By day, Sky holds a University Research Chair in Drama and Creative Writing at Guelph University.